KU-444-478

Hercules

OPERATION SNOWSEARCH

*Also by Peter Clover
published by Hodder Children's Books*

Hercules 1: New Pup on the Block
Hercules 3: Treasure Hound

Rescue Riders 1: Race Against Time
Rescue Riders 2: Fire Alert
Rescue Riders 3: Ghost Pony

PETER CLOVER

*Hodder
Children's
Books*

a division of Hodder Headline

For Vivia and Russell

A Catalogue record for this book is available from
the British Library

ISBN 0 340 75295 5

Typeset by Avon Dataset Ltd, Bidford-on-Avon, Warks

Printed and bound in Great Britain by
The Guernsey Press Co. Ltd, Channel Isles

Hodder Children's Books
A Division of Hodder Headline
338 Euston Road
London NW1 3BH

One

It started off like any other Saturday morning. Jack woke early at seven thirty, to the sound of the *Pacific Princess* passing through Sallyford village on its way to Rilport.

The old steam train didn't stop but sounded two long whistles as it rumbled through.

Awake, but still bleary-eyed, Jack patted

the folds of the duvet for signs of his little dog, Hercules.

But instead of Hercules' rough, shaggy coat against his hand, all Jack felt was soft cotton duvet. Sighing, Jack sat up. It could only mean one thing: Hercules was in his chest of drawers.

Each night, when Jack went to sleep, Hercules curled himself up in a ball at the foot of his bed.

Sometimes the little dog inched his way up on to Jack's pillow and slept with his tail curled around Jack's nose. And sometimes he made a cosy nest between Jack's legs and stayed there all night.

But if Jack ever left the drawers pulled out on his clothes chest, Hercules would make his bed amongst Jack's sweatshirts and jumpers, using the pulled-out drawers like steps to climb up to the top drawer to make a nest.

And that was exactly where Hercules

was. Sleeping and snoring in the top drawer!

Jack slipped out of bed and tiptoed across the room.

'Zzzzzzzzzzz.' The noise of a lazy dog snoring filled his ears. Hercules was curled up in a tight ball amongst Jack's clothes.

Jack blew on to Hercules' face. The little dog mumbled and stirred. Jack blew again, rippling the dog's wiry fringe. Hercules blinked his eyes, suddenly wide

awake and ready for anything.

Jack buried his face deep in Hercules' scrappy, doggy fur.

The little dog sat up immediately, and covered Jack with slobbery, good-morning kisses.

'Come on, lazy bones,' said Jack. He ruffled the little dog's ears and stared into the cute mutt's face.

Hercules stared back. He seemed to be saying, 'OK. What now?'

'I bet you've forgotten, haven't you?' said Jack.

'Forgotten?' Hercules didn't know what that word meant. But he knew enough to realise that his young master was excited about something.

'Next door!' said Jack.

Hercules still had no idea what Jack was on about. But he wagged his tail all the same, until it seemed that at any minute it might drop off.

'Don't you remember?' asked Jack. 'It's today! Our new neighbour is moving in today!'

'Wuff, wuff,' Hercules answered with a soft bark. He pushed his nose into Jack's face and poked his tongue into his master's soft pink ear. Jack grimaced, and went to have a wash.

It only took Jack five minutes to dress. He quickly made his bed, then chased Hercules down the stairs and into the kitchen for breakfast.

'Morning, Jack. Morning, Hercules,' smiled Mum. She threw more toast under the grill and opened a tin of dog meat for Hercules.

The little dog sniffed at his food bowl. The smell of toast seemed more appealing. Hercules hopped up on to a chair and placed his forepaws squarely on the kitchen table.

'No!' said Mum, sternly. But her face was smiling.

'Bad boy,' said Jack. But it meant nothing to Hercules. He could clearly see that they both looked happy. The little dog stayed where he was, and rested his hairy chin on his paws. Hercules' tail thumped the back of the chair as the toast under the grill turned a golden brown.

While they were having breakfast, a huge removal van pulled up next door. The new neighbour had arrived!

Jack peered through the kitchen curtains as the big removal lorry crunched to a halt on the gravel drive.

The lorry seemed to sit there for ages before anything happened.

Jack half expected a family with children to come bustling out of the lorry. Instead, a small red car pulled up alongside, and an elderly lady climbed out of the vehicle. In her arms she cradled a small, fluffy bundle.

The new neighbour walked briskly across

the front lawn and up into the house.

Jack strained his eyes for a better look at what she was holding. Hercules also pushed his nose against the glass. But all they could make out was a cloud of fluffy beige fur. It could have been anything.

But it wasn't anything. It was Bambi.

Bambi was a chihuahua. And Bambi belonged to Mrs Hutchens, the new neighbour.

Bambi shook her head from side to side and tried to wriggle free from the strong arms which held her fast. But Mrs Hutchens held on tightly and nursed her baby into the house.

At last Jack dragged his eyes away from the house next door. Mrs Hutchens was standing at the window now, cradling Bambi in her arms. Hercules still peered through his shaggy fringe, staring hard at the new arrivals.

Jack reached out with his hand and found

the exact spot between Hercules' ears which made him close his eyes.

Hercules flicked his head round. Two bright, intelligent eyes looked adoringly up at Jack. The little dog's nose felt moist and his tongue wet as he licked his master's hand.

'You want to go and make friends, don't you?' said Jack.

Hercules gave his answer with a soft bark. 'Wuff.'

'Well, you'll just have to wait,' grinned Jack.

'Give them a chance to settle in!'

It was much later in the morning when Jack finally decided to pop next door and say hello to the new neighbour.

The removal van had long since gone and the house seemed quiet, almost empty.

Jack led Hercules up the garden path on his lead. The little dog seemed very excited.

His tail waggled around as though it were on a spring. *Swish, swish, swish.* It beat against Jack's legs as he reached up and rang the doorbell. *Thump, thump, thump.* That tail never stopped.

At first, Jack thought there was no one at home. It seemed to take ages before the door creaked and swung open.

Mrs Hutchens stood on the door sill, peering cautiously over her spectacles.

'Yes?' she demanded curtly. 'What do you want?'

Jack could see Bambi, the little chihuahua, hiding behind her legs. Hercules could see Bambi, too, and lurched forward to say hello.

Before Jack could introduce himself, Mrs Hutchens screamed in alarm and slammed the door closed.

BANG!

'Oh dear,' said Jack. 'That didn't go very well, did it?' Hercules looked up and whined. He sniffed around the door frame, then raised a paw as if to say, 'What happened?'

'I don't think Mrs Hutchens wants Bambi to make friends,' said Jack.

Hercules sat down on his fat little legs and gave a series of short barks. Mrs Hutchens was standing at the window now with a frosty frown plastered across her face. She was cradling Bambi in her arms and mouthing shooing sounds.

'Go away,' she said. 'Go away!'

Jack could hear her muffled cries through the glass.

'Go away! And take that hairy sausage with you!'

'I think she wants us to leave,' said Jack. He ran a hand through his floppy blond hair and gave a short tug on Hercules' lead.

The little dog leaped sideways and trotted away down the garden path next to his young master.

'Come on, boy. We'll go for a nice long walk instead!'

Two

In the dull drizzle of the morning, Jack took Hercules up to the Widdenham Clumps, a candy-floss-shaped group of trees stuck into the top of the hill behind Bodkin's field.

From the summit of the hill, Jack and Hercules looked down across Sallyford, and beyond the fields and rooftops to a glittering mirror of sea and shingle shore.

They could see the railway track snaking

its way along the rocky coast and through the village before it disappeared into a hillside tunnel.

Jack checked his watch. There wouldn't be a train through for at least another half an hour. And the *Pacific Princess* steam engine wasn't due back until the afternoon. Jack decided to walk Hercules back down the hill and follow the hedgerow path around Bodkin Farm.

It had stopped raining now. Jack ruffled Hercules' neck and unclipped his lead. There was a nice run for the little dog along the wooded hedgerow.

'You might even get to chase a rabbit,' said Jack.

Hercules cocked his floppy ears and panted with his tongue lolling. He looked up at Jack, gave a sharp bark, then thundered off through the long wet grass on his little stumpy legs.

Jack watched him go like a rocket,

down the hill and away. He picked up a long stick and swished at the passing undergrowth as he walked.

He couldn't believe how fast his dog was. Within minutes, Hercules had disappeared from sight.

Jack looked around and scanned the rough, bumpy track ahead. But Hercules was nowhere to be seen.

'Hercules!' called Jack. He wasn't really worried, but didn't like his little dog being out of sight for too long.

Then Jack heard a frantic bark.

'Hercules! Is that you?' Jack hurried his pace, following the sound of urgent barking from up ahead. It seemed to be coming from inside the first run of thick hedging, only metres away. Jack knew it was Hercules.

Something was making him bark frantically and Jack was almost certain that it was a rabbit.

Jack didn't mind Hercules chasing rabbits

– it was good exercise for fat little dogs. But he didn't like the idea of Hercules actually *catching* one. Jack loved all animals and wouldn't want his dog ever to hurt anything. Concerned, Jack stumbled into the dense hawthorn hedge after Hercules.

'*There* you are!' cried Jack, snapping off a prickly twig which had caught on his jacket.

Hercules was running up and down inside a hollow section of the hedge, barking in alarm. Then he disappeared into a tunnel running beneath the bank and vanished completely.

'Hercules,' said Jack sternly. 'Come out!' He squatted down on all fours and peered into the muddy burrow.

Hercules lay flat on his belly, desperately pulling at something inside, trying to remove his find from the hole. Jack caught a glimpse of something brown and furry. Then he saw the shiny glint of copper wire. It was a dead rabbit, caught in a wire snare.

Jack's face clouded over with anger.

'OK, Hercules, take it easy. Here, boy. Come here.'

Hercules backed out of the burrow and watched as Jack reached inside and tried to release the rabbit from the vicious trap.

Jack carefully began to unwrap the wire caught around the rabbit's hindleg. Hercules had calmed down now and watched as his master set to work. The little dog panted and whined as Jack pulled out the dead rabbit. The wire snare had cut deeply into its leg and the brown fur was stained with blood. The poor thing had obviously died in great pain.

Jack rose to his feet and scowled at the wire snare dangling from his hand.

'These things are terrible!' he exclaimed.

Hercules gave a sharp bark of agreement. 'Wuff.' Then he scratched his ear with a vigorous paw.

Jack held up the wire. The noose which

had caught the rabbit was clearly visible at one end.

Jack knew that poachers sometimes set these nasty traps. He didn't think it could possibly be Mr Bodkin, the farmer. *Whoever set a snare like this*, thought Jack, *must know that any other animal which ran through the hedge would also get caught. Only someone who didn't care about animals would do something like that!*

Hercules nosed at the dead rabbit and poked at it with his wet muzzle. He looked up at Jack and raised a sad paw. Hercules thought it was awful, too!

Jack decided to take the rabbit, along with the snare, and show it to Mr Bodkin.

'If there's a poacher working the hedgerows,' Jack said to himself, 'then the farmer should be told.'

'Wuff, wuff,' agreed Hercules. He chased his tail in a circle before dashing off to lead Jack down to the farm.

Jack hurried along the track, anxious to show Mr Bodkin what he had found.

Hercules ran ahead into the farmyard barking his head off. He had never been to a farm before, but he liked the smell of the barns and all the different animals. The air was sweet with hay and the noise of sheep bleating in the back meadow. Hercules liked this new place very much.

And when Mr Bodkin rolled out from beneath his tractor to see what all the noise was about, Hercules immediately decided that he liked him too!

The little dog rolled on his back at the farmer's feet and waggled his legs in the air.

Mr Bodkin wiped his brow with the back of his hand, smearing black oil across his forehead.

'What's all this, then?' smiled the farmer. He looked down at the squirming dog, and bent to tickle Hercules' pink tummy.

Just then, Jack trotted into the yard with
the dead rabbit. Mr Bodkin had known Jack
since he was a baby. He was good friends
with Jack's father.

'Hello, Jack! What's that you've got
there?'

At first, the farmer didn't see the wire
snare. He only saw the rabbit.

But then his eyes narrowed and he

glowered at the gleaming wire in Jack's hand.

'Where did you get that from?' asked Mr Bodkin. He took the snare in his big hands as Jack told him exactly where he had found it.

'These things are lethal,' the farmer said. 'They're set by poachers for rabbits. But any small animals which get themselves caught in the hoop are trapped fast, until whoever set the snare comes back to finish them off.'

'That's horrible,' said Jack. 'How could anyone do that?' He caught hold of Hercules' collar and clipped on his lead.

'There's been a poacher up in the woods for at least a week or more,' said Mr Bodkin. 'But he's never dared to come this far down to the farm before. I've found traps and snares up in the Widdenham Clumps, and one in the hedgerow by the big field. But never one as close to home as this!'

Jack watched as the farmer destroyed the wire snare.

'I had one of my dogs and a young lamb caught in a similar trap last week,' the farmer continued. 'The daft things stepped in them and got caught. And the more they panicked and struggled, the tighter the snares became. The dog wasn't too badly injured but the poor lamb got itself into a right mess. It was terrible.'

Hercules was leaping up at Jack's legs now. Jack bent down and picked up his dog. Carefully cradling him in his arms. Just talking about the traps made him want to keep Hercules safe and out of harm's way.

'I thought only big country estates had trouble with poachers,' said Jack. 'I didn't realise that ordinary country people and farmers could have problems, too!'

'This poacher doesn't seem to care about anything,' replied Mr Bodkin. 'There's so much woodland and open countryside around here, he can come and go as he pleases. It's the ideal spot for his kind of trapping. But he's trampled crops with all his blundering about – as well as caused lots of animals unnecessary suffering.'

Jack decided right then that he wanted to help. He wanted to stop this poacher trapping and killing any more wild animals on the farmer's land. But, above all, he wanted this poacher to be caught before he harmed a domestic animal. Like an innocent dog. Like Hercules.

The farmer managed a smile. 'I wish I had the time,' he said, 'to search all the woods, all the fields, and all the hedgerows. Then I'd find his wicked snares and traps and drive him off my land once and for all!'

'Can't the police help?' asked Jack.

'They're far too busy for something like this,' sighed the farmer.

Hercules gave a loud bark.

'But we're not, are we, Hercules?' said Jack. 'We've got *heaps* of time. We've got a whole week of half-term with nothing to do but search for poacher's traps!'

Mr Bodkin raised his eyebrows. 'It's not that simple,' he said. 'It could be dangerous. And, with a dog, you'd have to be extra careful.'

'We'd be extra, *extra* careful, wouldn't we, boy?' grinned Jack, looking at Hercules.

'Well, if you *did* find any traps,' said the farmer, 'it would be a great help if you could destroy them.'

Jack cradled Hercules in his arms and rubbed his chin hard between the dog's ears.

'I bet we could find every single trap that's been set,' exclaimed Jack, confidently.

'It's not a job I'm offering,' said the farmer, 'but I'd willingly pay fifty pence for any trap found and brought here to the house.'

Jack grinned and offered his outstretched hand.

'It's a deal!'

Three

Jack and Hercules decided to begin their mission straight away, since they had the whole afternoon ahead of them.

Hercules flicked up both ears and his eyes twinkled beneath his scrubbing-brush fringe. The little dog seemed to know that something important was happening. He scrabbled his hairy paws in the muddy earth and sniffed at the frosty soil.

Hercules was on the case.

Jack started afresh back up on the Clumps. It was the highest spot in the area and the perfect place to begin checking for traps.

Jack decided to set himself different routes down the hill and investigate all the tracks and pathways through the woods and along the hedgerows.

It didn't take long before they found another trap.

The wire snare was hidden beneath a cover of winter leaves. Hercules took a mouthful of denim and tugged Jack to a standstill. His grip on Jack's jeans stopped Jack from placing his foot squarely into the wire noose.

The little dog growled and grumbled until Jack realised that Hercules was trying to show him something. Jack knelt down and brushed away the leaves covering the snare.

Hercules barked and danced around him as Jack destroyed the trap and held up the broken wire.

'That's *one*, boy,' said Jack, grinning. 'Let's see how many more you can find.'

Hercules bounded ahead excitedly, pushing his nose into the leafy drifts carpeting the pathway. Jack traipsed along behind, poking the bushes and undergrowth with his long stick. Crisp, frosty leaves were brushed aside, but Jack didn't find another poacher's snare until they reached the bottom of the hill.

A broad, thick hedge, similar to the one where Hercules had discovered the dead rabbit, ran alongside the west field. The little dog found an opening in the foliage and burrowed his way deep into the hedge. Once inside, there was a well-used run of at least a hundred metres, hidden within the spindly branches of the hedgerow.

Hercules found three more snares in there and burst out of the hedge, eager to show his master what he had found.

But when Jack looked inside, it wasn't very nice.

'Oh, no,' groaned Jack, as he crawled into the hole. He reached back carefully with his hand to take hold of Hercules' collar. 'Stay here, boy,' he ordered sternly. 'Stay!'

The little dog obeyed and plonked himself down on the ground. He gave a little whine as he watched the soles of Jack's trainers disappear into the hedge.

Inside the hedge, the first two snares Jack found were empty. Jack pulled at the wire traps and quickly destroyed them. He stuffed them into his jacket pocket, then crept forward towards the third trap.

This snare held another dead rabbit. It looked like it had been dead a long time. Jack pinched his nose and pulled a disgusted face, then reached for the wire holding the snare and dragged it out of the hedge.

Hercules jumped up at Jack as he crawled out on to the path, and started to lick Jack's face affectionately with a sloppy wet tongue.

'Gerroff,' complained Jack, weakly. He didn't really mind at all. And Hercules knew that. Which is why he didn't stop.

Once he was back on his feet, Jack held the rabbit well away from him. He held the wire and tried not to touch the poor dead creature. It was very smelly. But Hercules didn't mind. He raised himself up on his hindlegs and tried to sniff the rabbit's fur.

'No!' said Jack sternly. He held the rabbit further away. Jack didn't want Hercules anywhere near it. He decided to take the traps and the dead rabbit to Mr Bodkin straight away.

Mr Bodkin was pleased that Jack and Hercules had found and destroyed another four traps. But he was very angry to discover that the poacher was setting so many snares.

'I've just spent most of the afternoon rounding up my sheep and getting them all back into their field,' complained Mr Bodkin. 'The poacher obviously left the field gate open when he was out setting his traps. My sheep were all over the main road! Some were even wandering down to the village by the time I found out. It's taken me all this time to get them back in and settled.'

'We should report it to the police,' said Jack. 'They could set an ambush and catch this poacher red-handed.'

Mr Bodkin smiled weakly. 'I'm not the only one having problems with this poacher,' he said. 'Other farmers are complaining, too. But the police don't think it's serious enough to get involved.'

'Well, *we* think it's very serious, don't we, boy?' piped up Jack. The little dog answered with a soft bark.

'I think it's serious, too,' said the farmer. 'But the police don't have time to worry about a few dead rabbits. Most people think rabbits are pests, anyway.'

Suddenly Jack understood. To the police, a few dead rabbits didn't add up to much of a crime. And the poacher probably knew that. But, to the farmers, every little incident added up to one big problem. And Jack was determined that he and Hercules would help sort it out.

Jack thought of nothing else as he raced Hercules back across Bodkin's field and home.

As usual, Hercules won. His little stumpy legs could move so fast they became nothing but a grey blur. Hercules was a rocket on legs and, no matter how fast Jack ran, he just couldn't keep up.

Hercules burst into the kitchen with a scrabble of sharp claws on the polished floor tiles. Jack stumbled in several minutes later, puffing and blowing like Dad's old steam train, the *Pacific Princess*.

His mum shot a glance over her shoulder. She was washing up at the kitchen sink.

'I was wondering where you were,' she laughed. 'Hercules has been here for hours!'

The little dog jumped up at her legs and tried to attack the rubber gloves draped across the draining-board. The smell of chicken casserole filled his nostrils and Hercules was hoping for something special to eat.

'Open a tin of dog food and feed the mighty midget,' laughed Mum. Hercules plonked himself down and pressed his belly on to the warm floor tiles in front of the Aga. He watched Jack open a tin of his favourite food, before wolfing the lot as soon as it was set down in front of him.

Then, as Jack told his mum all about their afternoon and the poacher's traps, Hercules sneaked outside to see if he could spot Bambi, his new doggy neighbour.

What with all the business of dead rabbits and poachers, Jack seemed to have forgotten all about his new neighbour. But Hercules hadn't. He scampered up to the hedge and sniffed around at the base of the thick privet.

Jack glanced out of the window and saw Hercules scraping and digging away at the roots and earth.

'Look at that crazy dog,' said Jack. 'He thinks there's a poacher's snare hidden in our hedge!'

But Hercules was thinking nothing of the sort. Hercules was busy tunnelling into next door's garden.

Four

Earth and mud flew everywhere as Hercules scrabbled away with his front paws. It didn't take very long. The ground was cold and hard, but it fell away in big frosty clumps.

The little dog soon had a perfect burrow leading directly from his garden into the garden next door.

Hercules sniffed the air. It smelled cold

and icy as if there was snow about to fall. He looked back at Jack standing at the cottage window, then, before his owner could stop him, Hercules darted through the tunnel he'd just made, and surfaced in Mrs Hutchens' garden next door.

He hesitated, then looked up at the new neighbour's cottage.

Somewhere inside that house was Bambi. He knew they could be friends – if only he could get to meet her!

He looked at the white-washed walls and the green ivy, which crept its way up and over the front porch. Then he noticed that all the windows on the ground floor, despite the cold weather, were wide open.

Hercules looked hard. He studied each window in turn.

'Wuff!' Yes! There she was. Bambi was sitting on a window seat in the lounge, peering out into the garden with her nose twitching as she sniffed the air.

Hercules ran forward, excitedly. His tail wagged and drummed the neighbour's lawn. He looked up at the little chihuahua in the window and made whining noises in his throat. Then he stretched his body like elastic, and reached up with his forepaws to touch the windowsill.

Bambi edged forward, instantly alert.

Hercules stretched a little further. Their noses were only a few centimetres apart. Hercules sighed in anticipation. Then it happened. Bambi snapped her jaws and nipped Hercules right on the tip of his nose.

'Yowwll!' Hercules yelped with pain, then turned tail and shot across the lawn and back down through the burrow. He surfaced in his own garden, right by Jack's feet. Jack looked down at him in surprise.

'Hercules. What on earth have you been up to?' Jack could see the bloodied nose and the hurt look in his dog's eyes.

Then he noticed the tunnel burrowed beneath the hedge.

'Oh, I *see*,' grinned Jack. 'Trying to make friends with the new neighbours, eh? You don't seem to have got off to a very good start, do you?'

Hercules raised a paw and scratched at Jack's jeans.

'Never mind. Come on, silly. I think that nose needs a plaster.'

Jack led Hercules back to the cottage. The little dog padded along behind him with his tail tucked between his legs. Jack sat Hercules on a kitchen chair while he dabbed at his dog's nose with cotton wool. He tried to stick a plaster across the wound, but it

wouldn't stay put for more than a second. Hercules was too hairy and it kept falling off.

Poor Hercules. He felt awful. He just wanted to hide himself away under Jack's bed and sleep off his embarrassment. He wouldn't even come out to say goodnight when Jack came up to bed.

But when Jack woke up in the morning, the little hairy mongrel was curled up in his arms, nestling amongst the folds of the soft, cosy duvet.

Jack ruffled the squidgy ears which flopped across his face, and tickled the soft pink belly squirming beneath his hand.

'Good morning, Hercules,' he groaned lazily. It was still very early and the bedroom felt cold and chilly. But it was snug and warm in bed. Jack pulled the duvet up over his head and held on to the sides to stop Hercules trying to burrow his way inside.

Jack held on fast, but the little dog was very determined. Within seconds he had poked his nose through an opening and wormed his way inside the bedding to curl up next to his young master.

Jack giggled. 'No, Hercules – get out!' He poked Hercules in the ribs but it had no effect. Hercules just buried his head further under the duvet and ignored him.

'Come on.' Jack poked again. This time Hercules rolled over and grabbed a corner of duvet in his jaws. Then he fell off the bed, on to the floor, dragging the duvet with him.

'Brrrr! It's freezing!' Jack tried to grab at the duvet before it disappeared completely, but he was too late. Hercules had already made a nest out of it on the floor.

'I guess it's time to get up, then,' said Jack resignedly.

Jack wrapped himself up in his dressing

gown and wandered sleepily into the bathroom for a quick wash and brush-up.

Jack could hear Hercules snoring loudly in the bedroom as he got himself ready.

It's all right for dogs, he thought. They *don't have to wash and dress. They just have to wake up.*

Suddenly he heard Hercules bark. Jack headed back to his room. He was amazed at how Hercules could be asleep one minute, and the next, sitting by the bedroom window barking. He looked out to see what the fuss was about.

'Bambi!' exclaimed Jack. The little chihuahua was in their garden, sniffing around the flower-beds along the hedge.

'She must have come through that tunnel you dug yesterday,' Jack said, smiling at Hercules. 'Look at her. She's having a really good nose around.'

Hercules squashed his nose up against the windowpane and gave three soft 'wuffs'.

Then he howled sharply as the glass rubbed against his sore nose.

'I think I should get downstairs and return Bambi to Mrs Hutchens,' said Jack. 'You'd better stay here, boy.' Hercules cocked his head to one side and whimpered, as if to say 'Can't I come too?'.

Jack shook his head at his little dog, then threw on a thick sweatshirt and jeans and hurried downstairs. Outside in the garden, Bambi was shaking the life out of a ferocious crisp packet she had found. The tiny dog was really enjoying herself, growling and snarling like a pint-sized Rottweiler.

Suddenly she saw Jack. Dropping the crisp packet, the tiny chihuahua bared her teeth and yap, yap, yapped for all she was worth. She was shaking from head to tail and looked very nervous.

Jack crouched down on the grass and tried to make himself seem smaller, less

threatening. He reached out and offered the back of his hand for Bambi to sniff.

The tiny dog froze. She looked so little and helpless. Jack wondered what to do next. Should he risk a nip and try to pick Bambi up? Or should he call Mrs Hutchens and abandon any attempts to return Bambi himself?

Before he could decide, Hercules burst on to the scene. He rushed up to Bambi and skidded to a halt, centimetres away from her front paws. Then he rolled over on to his back and tapped at the chihuahua playfully with a gentle paw.

Bambi made a noise which sounded like a hiccup. Then she looked up at Jack with eyes that seemed to say, 'OK, you can pick me up now. I won't bite.'

Bambi seemed much happier when she was up off the ground, cradled in Jack's arms, far away from the attentions of the boisterous Hercules.

'You stay here, boy. I'll take Bambi home,' said Jack. Hercules pricked up his ears like a rabbit. He watched as Jack carried Bambi through the cottage gate, out into the lane and into next door's garden.

But Hercules didn't want to be left out of anything. He dived through the tunnel beneath the hedge and appeared like magic on the neighbour's patch of lawn.

Bambi gave an excited yap. She thought that this was great fun.

Just then Mrs Hutchens appeared at the open door, her nose pinched and her lips thin. She took one look at Bambi in Jack's arms and started yelling.

'My baby! What are you doing with my baby?' She lurched forward and snatched the chihuahua out of Jack's arms.

'You're trying to steal my baby,' she screeched accusingly.

Hercules chose that moment to jump up at his frosty neighbour and try to take a lick at Bambi's feet.

'Get him off!' screamed Mrs Hutchens. 'You nasty animal,' she shouted at Hercules. 'And you nasty child,' she said to Jack. 'You wait until your parents hear about this!'

Then she stormed inside and slammed the door shut.

'And keep out of my garden,' she yelled through the letterbox.

Jack hugged himself and shivered in the cold as the first snowflakes fell from the wintry sky. 'What a rotten neighbour,' he mumbled.

Five

The next day was a surprise for everyone. The snow had been falling for most of the night, and when Jack woke up and peered through his bedroom window all he could see was a blanket of white covering the entire countryside. All the rooftops and cottage chimney pots were covered with snow. And the ground was fresh, crisp and white.

Hercules nuzzled his way between Jack's arms and looked out through the window, down into the garden. Everything down there was white and frosty, too!

Hercules had never seen snow before. He raced downstairs, eager to scratch and scrape at the back door. He couldn't wait to get outside to investigate.

Jack was close behind him, wrapped in his warmest clothes. He opened the door and Hercules shot out like a bullet.

The soft snow fell away beneath the little dog's short stumpy paws. And Hercules was soon up to his tummy in soft white snow.

'Brrr!' Jack shivered. It was cold outside. But the sky was blue and the sun was shining. It was still a brilliant day for a walk – and for hunting down poachers' snares hidden beneath the hedgerows.

After breakfast, Jack clipped on Hercules'

collar and led him outside. Hercules pulled on his lead and tried to drag Jack across the lawn to the hedge dividing their garden from the one next door.

'No,' said Jack sternly. 'You're not going through that tunnel again. Bambi doesn't want to be friends. And neither does Mrs Hutchens.'

Jack parted the hair that drooped over the little dog's face. Two bright intelligent eyes looked up at him.

'I'm sorry,' said Jack. 'But from now on, next door is out of bounds. No more visits. No more Bambi!'

Hercules flopped his ears and looked really sad. The snow came up to his tummy and tipped his whiskery chin with frost.

'Come on,' soothed Jack. 'Give it a week or two and then you can try again. Making friends can sometimes take time!'

Hercules leaped up and wagged his tail. Then he took a bite at the soft snow and howled at the cold, icy taste in his mouth.

'I'll take you for a nice long walk,' said Jack. 'I shouldn't think you'll catch sight of Bambi until all this snow melts anyway!'

Hercules shook his coat and showered Jack with snowflakes. Then he bounded towards the gate, pulling the lead out of Jack's hands.

'Wait!' called a voice from over the hedge. It was Mrs Hutchens.

Oh, no! thought Jack. He stopped in his tracks, expecting a telling-off. Hercules hid between his legs.

'Have you seen my Bambi?' she cried. 'Have you seen her? You've got to help me find my baby!'

Jack didn't know what to think. One minute Mrs Hutchens was ordering him to

keep away, and the next she was asking for his help.

Hercules peered at Mrs Hutchens through Jack's legs.

'Well, have you seen her?' Mrs Hutchens repeated.

'Err, no,' replied Jack nervously. He was worried in case he said the wrong thing. 'I haven't seem Bambi since yesterday.'

'Well, she's gone missing,' exclaimed Mrs Hutchens. 'And I expect it's all your fault! That dog of yours has frightened her away.'

Jack couldn't believe what he was hearing. *He* hadn't done anything wrong. Yet, as he watched his neighbour traipse back to her cottage, he suddenly felt sad. And realised how unfair it was. Not just to him, but to Mrs Hutchens. She had only just moved to Sallyford, and after one day her precious dog had disappeared.

She must feel awful. She had no friends nearby. No one to talk to. All she had was the horrible empty feeling of losing her pet. Her beloved Bambi.

It must be rotten, thought Jack, remembering how worried he had been when Hercules had gone missing. He made up his mind there and then to go out and search for Bambi. He was taking Hercules for a walk anyway. If the little chihuahua was out there, then Jack

and Hercules would find her. They had to. Bambi wouldn't last long in all that freezing snow.

They didn't have a minute to lose. Bambi's life depended on them finding her!

Jack was in the kitchen telling Mum what had happened.

'Do you think Hercules really *did* frighten Bambi away?' Jack asked.

'No, I don't think so at all,' said Mum. She sounded quite certain about this. 'Mrs Hutchens probably left the gate open and Bambi just wandered off. That little dog's been so pampered, she would probably get lost quite easily, anywhere on her own. And in a strange place, with all this snow, getting totally lost would be very easy.'

'Poor Bambi,' said Jack. 'She won't know anything about crossing roads or keeping away from the railway track.'

'Or the river,' added Mum.

'What if she's been knocked down and is lying injured somewhere?' said Jack. 'Or worse, caught in a poacher's snare!'

'Mrs Hutchens must be feeling terrible,' said Mum. 'I'll go next door and tell her that you and Hercules are going out searching.'

Hercules flicked up his ears when he heard his name and raised a front paw as if to say, 'Come on, then. Let's go!'

They searched for nearly three hours, but there was no trace of Bambi. Hercules found two more traps: one tucked away in the hedge levelling Bodkin's field, and another just at the end of the lane in the Dollip ditch. That one was just a bit too close to home.

'It's getting really cold,' said Jack, unwinding his scarf from his neck as he strode back into the warm kitchen. 'And the sky's full of fresh snow, too,' he added.

Hercules threw himself at Mum and dried his soggy paws on her thick woolly skirt.

'Gerroff,' she laughed, shifting her leg and stirring the thick soup she was making. But Hercules wouldn't quit until he got a cuddle and a dog-biscuit.

'You just won't take no for an answer, will you?' grinned Mum. Hercules drooped his eyelids and looked pathetic. Then he snaffled the biscuit and offered his paw in return for another.

Mum ignored him. She looked up at the sky, through the kitchen window. It didn't look good. The horizon was heavy with yellow-grey snow clouds.

Jack's heart sank. 'If it snows again, this afternoon, then Bambi won't stand a chance,' he said. 'She's got hardly any coat, not like Hercules. And I'm really worried about those traps . . .'

Jack had a sudden vision of Bambi lying shivering and frozen somewhere out in the snow.

'Why don't you pop next door and talk to Mrs Hutchens,' said Mum. 'Tell her you've been searching all morning. You never know; maybe Bambi's come back!'

But Jack wasn't optimistic. Nevertheless, he went next door. And Hercules followed. Jack knocked at the front door.

'What are *you* doing here?' said Mrs Hutchens angrily. 'And what are you doing bringing round that mongrel of a dog? He should be locked away after what he did to Bambi.'

Jack was furious but he tried to stay calm.

'Honestly, Mrs Hutchens,' he said. 'I really don't think Hercules was responsible for scaring Bambi away.'

Mrs Hutchens glowered at both Jack and Hercules. Her face seemed frozen, cold and hard like the weather. But, behind her glasses, Mrs Hutchens' eyes were red and full of tears. Her stony face suddenly crumpled as she pressed a hand to her lips.

'Well, maybe you *are* right,' she said. 'But Bambi's still missing and there's no reason I can think of that would have made her run away.'

'Perhaps she's just gone exploring,' said Jack. 'Most dogs like to explore.'

'Not Bambi,' snapped Mrs Hutchens tearfully. Then she ran back into the cottage without another word.

Jack felt dreadful.

'Poor Mrs Hutchens,' he said. 'She must really love Bambi. I guess she's not such a witch, after all. Anyone who cares for a dog that much can't be all bad.'

Jack shivered where he stood and glanced up at the sky again. It was getting colder by the minute, and the snow was banking in the clouds, preparing to fall. *If Bambi's lying caught in a trap*, thought Jack, *then she won't last the night!*

He looked at his watch, then down at Hercules. It was just after one o'clock. 'Come on, boy. Let's grab a bite to eat and warm up a bit. Then we'll have another look for Bambi. This afternoon could be the last chance we get!'

Six

Jack changed into his warmest jacket and pulled a fur-lined tracker hat down over his ears. Then he took his best scarf and wrapped it round his neck three times.

'You look like an explorer about to trek across the Antarctic,' said Mum. She poured hot chocolate into a flask and packed it into a canvas field bag with some digestive biscuits. 'You'd better take this with you if you're going out again.'

Jack mumbled something through the thick layers of woolly scarf, which sounded like 'Thunannks!' and Hercules jumped up, trying to get at the biscuits in the bag.

'Don't stay out too long,' warned Mum. 'I don't like the look of those clouds.' She popped her mobile phone into Jack's bag. 'And ring if you find anything. Don't go being a hero in this weather. All you can do is look. Now, off you go. And be careful!'

As Jack and Hercules stepped outside, the first fresh fall of snowflakes began to drift down from the sky. Hercules snapped at the white frosty flakes and startled himself as they tingled coldly, dancing lightly on his warm tongue.

The snow made Hercules really playful. He strained on his lead and pulled Jack along at a swift pace.

'OK, boy, think,' mumbled Jack through his layers of scarf. 'If you were Bambi,

where would *you* go?'

The little dog cocked his head to one side and looked up and down the lane. Then, up to his chest in snow, he bounded across the road and headed off towards the little, stone pack-horse bridge spanning the stream.

Jack was happy to let Hercules lead the way this time. After all, who could be better at guessing where a missing dog might run off to than another dog?

Hercules barked as he ran ahead, sniffing and poking his snout into frozen holes and under snow-laden bushes.

A footpath led down from the bridge and followed the bubbling stream as it wound its way through the woodland. Finally the stream joined the river at Watersmeet, where the snow-covered banks rose steeply on both sides to channel a foaming waterfall.

Jack sat down on a fallen log and poured himself a cup of hot chocolate from the flask

Mum had packed. Hercules jumped up and settled himself on Jack's lap.

'I expect you'll want one of these,' teased Jack, waving a digestive biscuit in front of his dog.

'Wuff, wuff,' answered Hercules.

'Or maybe two! As you've been such a good boy.'

Hercules wasn't going to argue with that!

He quickly crunched two biscuits and was just trying to snaffle a third when a huge snowflake landed on his nose. Then another. And another.

'Here it comes,' said Jack. He glanced up at the sky, which was about to throw down a blizzard.

Hercules looked up too, and gave a sharp whine.

'It's all right, boy. Don't worry. We're going home now.' Jack ruffled his dog's shaggy head lovingly, to reassure him. But Hercules wasn't worried about the snow.

His sharp ears had picked up something else.

Someone moaning. Someone in trouble. And someone not very far away.

Suddenly, Jack heard it, too. He sprung up and turned to face the direction he thought the noise was coming from.

The snow was falling steadily now and a sudden flurry of icy flakes stung Jack's eyes and filled his mouth.

'*Pffuth, pffuth.*' Jack blew his mouth clear and wiped his eyes clean.

Hercules was barking continuously now and strained on his lead before diving head first into a nearby gully.

Whoever was in trouble had heard the barking and was now calling for help.

Jack unclipped Hercules' lead and let him run off through the snow to investigate.

'Go on, boy. Go find!'

The little dog bounded off behind some bushes and disappeared down into the steep gully which ran beside the river.

The snow-filled gully seemed to swallow Hercules up, and for a moment Jack panicked.

'Hercules!' he yelled, rushing over to peer down the steep bank.

The little dog answered with a soft 'Wuff'. He was at the bottom of the gully licking the face of a teenage boy. The boy was hanging upside down with one limp foot caught in a wire snare.

He couldn't pull himself up, and he couldn't move. The poor lad was trapped.

'Help,' moaned the youth. Being upside down for so long had given him a terrible headache.

'Don't worry,' called Jack. 'I'll soon have you up from there.'

The snow continued to fall fiercely as Jack took a deep breath and slid down the sloping wall of the gully on his backside. He landed squarely on the bottom, up to his knees in a snowdrift. From there, Jack climbed up to reach the wire snare around the youth's ankle. The wire had taken the weight of the lad's body and had cut deep into his flesh. His ankle didn't look very nice at all.

Jack decided to leave that part of the snare alone and concentrate on the other end of the wire. The end wire was attached to a peg and hammered into the gully wall beneath the snow. It was just like all the other traps that Jack and Hercules had destroyed.

He wiggled the peg really hard, backwards and forwards, until it gave way and set the wire free. The boy groaned and slid to the bottom of the gully. The snare was still attached to his ankle, but at least he was free.

Before Jack jumped down to help, he glanced up to where the snare had been set. It puzzled Jack as to why anyone would want to set a snare on such a steep bank.

Then he saw the drainpipe sticking out. The pipe ran right through the bank to the level of the river on the other side. Jack guessed that in heavy rain, if the river ever flooded, then the pipe would drain the extra water away safely into the gully.

But there was no water today. *The only thing running through that pipe*, thought Jack, *would be a rabbit or some other small animal*. Jack shuddered. That was exactly what the trap was there for.

He began to wonder how the teenage boy had got his foot caught in the first place.

But before he could figure it out, the youth grabbed Jack's leg and pulled him down into the gully beside him.

'You've got to help me get out of here,' he snapped gruffly.

Hercules jumped around at their feet and growled, as the boy used Jack's shoulder to support his weight.

'We don't have to climb up,' he said. 'Fifty metres along, this gully levels out and runs straight on to the riverbank.'

Jack was impressed at the stranger's knowledge. He had obviously been to this area before.

Hercules was happy to trot along behind, leaping in and out of the deep snowdrifts. The snow showed no sign of stopping.

The youth dragged his leg. It looked really painful. He told Jack that his name was Spider. 'I've been living rough in the countryside since I lost my job at the holiday camp in Rilport,' he confessed.

Jack felt sorry for Spider. He seemed nice.

But the more they spoke, as they forced their way through the blizzard, the more Jack realised that something wasn't quite right. And it had a lot to do with poachers' snares.

As they struggled along up the bank

and on to the river footpath, Hercules kept leaping up at Spider. The little dog was very interested in the contents of Spider's big jacket pockets.

'Gerroff!' snapped Spider, pushing Hercules away. But the little dog was more determined than Spider could have imagined. He kept snatching and nipping at the big pockets until finally he ripped one clean open. And out spilled a tight coil of copper wire. The kind used for making traps and snares.

Seven

Jack stared down at the bundle of wire. Hercules stared too. So did Spider. The wind whipped the snow into a thick white curtain, which made everything around them seem invisible.

All Jack could see was Hercules and the snare wire at their feet.

'I know what you're thinking,' said Spider. 'And you're right. I have been setting rabbit traps all over the place. I've been living rough for weeks and trapping was the only way I could think of to make some money.'

Jack looked puzzled.

'People pay good money for rabbit meat,' explained Spider. 'The butcher's shops can't get enough of it this time of year. It was the only way I could think of to survive. I know it was wrong.'

Jack didn't say a word. Spider leaned on his shoulder and they hobbled along in silence.

'I know you don't believe me,' Spider went on. 'But I was desperate. I'd lost my job and I had no choice.'

'It's cruel,' said Jack at last. 'Trapping animals that way is really cruel.' He wasn't sure if he liked Spider now, even though he was injured and needed help. 'It doesn't matter how desperate you are,' Jack added. 'You should never hurt or trap an animal like that.'

'OK, OK,' said Spider. 'I'm sorry. I really am. But at least now I know what it feels like to be caught in a snare. It's really painful. I was climbing out of the gully after setting some traps when I slipped. And I'd still be there now if it wasn't for you and that scrappy dog of yours.'

'He's not scrappy,' said Jack. 'That's Hercules. He's a star!'

'*Hercules*!' laughed Spider. 'That's the kind of name you give to a big hero, not a tatty, moth-eaten mongrel' Spider didn't mean to sound unkind. He just had a way of saying the wrong thing at the wrong time.

Jack was really cross. Just because Hercules was small and fat and scruffy didn't mean that he was rubbish. Hercules was the best dog in the whole world.

'Hercules,' called Jack. 'Here, boy.'

He slapped his leg and whistled, but there was no response. 'Hercules!' Jack called again. But suddenly there was no sign of his little dog.

They were almost at the village now. Jack wanted to shrug off Spider and run back to look for Hercules. But Spider's ankle was making him cry out in pain and his face was turning a funny shade of green.

Jack hoped that Hercules was following. The snowfall was now a full blizzard and the going was really difficult. Spider hung on grimly as they stumbled into the high street. The snow whipped itself into a frenzy and stung Jack's eyes. He didn't know what to do. He wanted to throw off the young poacher and run back to look for his dog. But the weather was making it impossible to do anything but head for home.

Then, suddenly, as they hit the village, Spider disappeared.

One minute he was there clinging on to Jack, and the next moment he was gone.

Perhaps it was the 'Police' sign above the

station door, thought Jack. Or the warning to poachers posted in the post office window. Whatever it was, Jack would never know for certain. All he did know was that he was standing in the middle of a snowstorm, alone.

Jack called for Hercules. He yelled and

whistled as loud as he could. But there was no sign of his little dog.

'Here, boy. Hercules! Come on, boy.' It was pointless. There was no sign of him. And the snow was falling so heavily now that Jack had no choice but to trudge home alone.

Mum was really pleased to see Jack. She had been worried about him out in the blizzard and was just about to go out looking for him herself.

When she heard that Hercules was missing, she was very concerned.

'I'm sure he'll find his own way home,' she said. 'He probably stopped off to explore a bush or a tree-trunk or something. Don't worry, Jack. Hercules will be scraping at the door at any moment. Just you wait and see.'

But Hercules didn't come scraping at the door. Hercules didn't come at all. And, even after the tea things had been cleared away and washed and dried, the little dog was still missing.

'I won't sleep a wink tonight,' said Jack, tearfully. 'The thought of Hercules out there in all that snow will give me nightmares.'

And he was right. All through the long night, Jack tossed and turned. He thumped his pillow a million times. And he hugged it a million times too. All his thoughts were aimed at Hercules. *Where was he? Where was his little hero?*

Jack had just slipped into a deep sleep when his alarm clock went off. It was morning. He sat bolt upright in his bed with a sudden start. His heart was thumping. It felt horrible. Especially when Jack looked down at the bedclothes and saw that there was no snoring Hercules beside him.

Outside, fresh snow drifted lazily against the windowpane. As Jack watched, the snowflakes got heavier and heavier. Great big fat flakes swirled and whirled as they settled themselves on to the ground.

Jack shivered. 'I can't bear to think about it,' he sighed to himself. 'Hercules is missing and I don't have a clue as to where he is!'

Suddenly, Jack's heart sank. He felt sick and sad. But he quickly got himself dressed and hurried downstairs, hoping madly that somehow Hercules had found his way home and was right now curled up in his cardboard box next to the Aga.

But as Jack hurried into the kitchen, his hopes were dashed. Hercules' box lay there, empty and cold.

Jack wanted to wake his mum and dad. He wanted to tell them just how sad he felt.

But it was still early and he knew he shouldn't disturb them.

Instead, he wrapped himself up in his warm jacket and wound his thick scarf round his head, topping the lot off with his trapper's hat.

He glanced at his watch. It was eight o'clock.

As Jack pushed open the back door, a flurry of snow swept into the kitchen. Jack bowed his head and pushed himself forward into the deep drift which had settled over the doorstep.

He quickly glanced across the garden to the hedge dividing the two gardens. A bit of Hercules' fur was sticking to a twig. It made Jack feel funny seeing it. But it made him more determined than ever to find his little dog.

Eight

Jack concentrated his thoughts, and pictured the last time he saw Hercules in his mind. It was like watching a video. He played the scene over and over inside his head.

Hercules was bounding along next to a belt of trees down by the river at Watersmeet. *Any tracks would be well covered by now*, thought Jack. But at least he had an idea where to look first.

He trudged on, knee-deep in snow, down the garden path and out into the lane. The morning breeze was crisp and cutting and the air felt sharp against Jack's nose and ears. Even through his scarf his breath made puffs of steam in the frosty air.

Shouting, calling, whistling for Hercules, Jack hurried on. Hoping against hope that the little dog would hear and answer with a bark.

The snow continued to fall, and an icy wind whipped at Jack's face, sticking snowflakes to his frozen cheeks. But still he marched on. No way was he going to quit until he had found Hercules.

Jack's boots crunched through the snowy drifts all the way down to the river. The air was thick and visibility was poor. It was like looking through a thick mist.

'What was that?' said Jack, suddenly.

He whistled again and called out Hercules'
name.

He had definitely heard something.

A soft barking sound came from
somewhere between the trees. 'Wuff, wuff,
wuff.'

It was unmistakable. It was Hercules. Jack
would have known that bark anywhere.

The going was tough, but Jack flew along, leaping and jumping with giant bounds across the snow-covered ground. He followed the sound of barking, and let Hercules' voice lead him forward.

Jack stopped, and looked around trying to locate where the barking was coming from.

He cupped his hands to his mouth and called again. 'Hercules! Hercules!'

Stumbling in the deep, soft snow, Jack plodded on towards a copse of trees, tripping over snow-hidden roots as he went.

The snow was falling so thickly now that it took Jack several seconds to make out a grey shape, curled in the hollow of some twisted tree roots. The old tree was a metre or two above the riverbank. Thick snow lay piled up against its gnarled trunk. But there, lying in the protective hollow of its roots, sheltering as best he could from the bitter cold, was Hercules.

'Hercules,' yelled Jack. 'Hercules! I'm here, boy. I'm here!'

Jack clambered over to the tree and dropped into the dry hollow. Puffing and panting from the effort of his climb, he wiped his hand across his eyes as he looked down at Hercules.

The snowflakes blurred his sight, but Jack thought he noticed something else, nestling against Hercules' fur.

He looked again, unable to believe his eyes.

Hercules lay curled in a tight ball within the shelter of the tree roots. His scrubbing-brush fringe bristled with encrusted snow, and his scrappy front paws were crossed to cover his nose. But his long body was curved protectively around something. Cuddling something close against his warm fur.

As Jack reached him, Hercules raised his head. The little dog whimpered softly, then

turned to lick the small head nestling against his body.

'It's Bambi!' breathed Jack softly. 'You're safe, boy. And you've got Bambi with you!'

Jack patted Hercules lovingly. His coat was thick with snow and stiff with ice. Jack fondled the little dog's ears and stroked the wiry hair along his neck down to his back.

Although it was still freezing, Hercules felt warm and cosy. Bambi seemed fine, too. Jack checked her out. She trembled as he touched her, and snuggled deeper into Hercules' fur. But Bambi was OK.

Then Jack noticed that something was wrong. Hercules was lying awkwardly. And, as Jack ran his hand round his dog's body, he felt something caught around his leg. It felt like wire.

'Oh no!' groaned Jack. Hercules was caught in a poacher's trap.

Jack checked again. The little dog whimpered with pain. The wire snare had cut deep into his leg. Yet, all this time, Hercules had lain quite still with the little chihuahua curled up safe and warm against his furry tummy. And he had stayed like that all through the long, cold night.

Hercules licked the back of Jack's hand as he stroked the dog's snow-matted chest.

'Don't worry, boy,' soothed Jack. 'I'll soon get you home. You must be freezing.' He used his scarf to rub Hercules' coat free of ice. 'We'll soon get that wire off and get you a nice big breakfast!'

But unfortunately it wasn't going to be that easy. Although Hercules was being very brave, and lying very still, there was no way he was going to be able to walk.

Nine

'I'll have to carry you,' said Jack. He left the snare around his dog's leg and yanked the wire roughly from its stake. Then he cradled Hercules gently in his arms.

Bambi stood shivering at Jack's feet. The poor thing had hardly any hair, her coat was so smooth. And the snow came almost up to her neck.

'Hang on a minute, boy!' Jack lowered

Hercules carefully on to the snow. Then he picked up Bambi and tucked her inside his jacket. 'Come on. We're all ready now.'

Hercules gave a soft 'Wuff' as Jack lifted him up again and they set off on the long haul home. Then he closed his eyes and fell fast asleep, with his shaggy head resting safely in the crook of his master's arm.

Bambi whimpered from inside Jack's jacket. She lay there, snug and happy to be out of the cold. But she was a very frightened dog. And she was quite sure that she would never go off exploring on her own again.

Jack's mum saw him struggling down the snow-carpeted lane from an upstairs window. At first she wondered what he was carrying. Then she saw Hercules and hurried downstairs.

Mrs Singer ran out into the snow-covered garden and stood there, not able to believe her eyes. Not only was Hercules bundled into Jack's arms, but a funny little face was peering out through his jacket.

'Bambi!' gasped Mum. The little head shot back and disappeared into the warm folds of Jack's coat.

'Come on. Into the house,' she urged. 'I'll get warm towels and some food.'

Within minutes they were settled round the kitchen range. The two dogs were huddled together once more, in a big cosy,

blanketed cardboard box, in front of the open fire.

Mum appeared with two thick bath towels and gave both dogs a good rubdown. She was careful not to touch Hercules' bad leg.

Bambi protested at first with rumbling growls, but soon gave in to the nice warm feeling of the towels.

Both dogs began to look more like themselves as the heat from the fire warmed them through.

'How about popping next door and telling Mrs Hutchens the good news about Bambi?' said Mum. 'I'll phone the vet and get someone to come and check them both over, and take this wire off Hercules. I don't fancy trying it myself. It looks pretty nasty.'

Hercules raised his head when he heard his name, then gave a pained whimper. Bambi shot up and began licking Hercules' whiskers. She pushed her face up close to her hero's and whimpered along with him.

Jack dashed next door and broke the news to their new neighbour. The old lady's cold eyes turned from hard frosty diamonds to warm blue pools, overflowing with tears.

'Bambi! My darling Bambi. Oh, you dear boy.' She brushed away the tears with her hand and laughed as she pulled on her coat. 'Oh, I can't tell you how grateful I am, Jack. If it wasn't for you and that brave little dog of yours . . .'

Before she could break into fresh sobs, Jack led her outside, and they hurried next door.

As they stepped into the kitchen, Mum was just putting the phone down. She looked upset.

'What is it?' asked Jack.

'The vet,' said Mum worriedly. 'He's out on an emergency call. It could be several hours before he gets here.'

'But *this* is an emergency,' exclaimed Jack. 'Poor Hercules is in agony. He needs help *now!*'

Mrs Hutchens was cradling Bambi in her arms and covering the tiny dog with kisses.

'Perhaps *I* can do something,' she smiled shyly. 'I was a veterinary nurse for twenty years before I retired. I'd like to help.'

Jack's mouth hung open in surprise.

Mrs Hutchens passed Bambi to Jack and knelt down to look at Hercules.

'I'll need a bowl of hot water and a clean tea towel,' she said. 'Disinfectant, too, if you have any. And a bandage.'

Mrs Hutchens examined the snare around Hercules' hindleg. It was very tight and the wire had cut right through his fur to the skin. It had been like that all night and was very sore.

Hercules closed his eyes and tried to be extra brave as Mrs Hutchens carefully removed the snare. He flinched once but he didn't moan or yelp.

Mrs Hutchens was very gentle. She cleaned and bathed Hercules' wound with hot water and disinfectant. Then she dressed it with a light bandage, ready for the vet when he arrived.

'There!' said Mrs Hutchens when she had finished. 'It's not quite as bad as it looks. Hercules was very clever to just lie there and not struggle.'

'Struggling makes the snares tighter,' said Jack.

'That's right,' said Mrs Hutchens. 'It could have been a lot worse. He's a brave little dog, and I can't thank him enough for finding and saving my Bambi.'

'Yip, yap,' agreed the little chihuahua. Bambi was glad that Hercules had found her, too. She seemed to have developed a soft spot for Jack's scruffy mongrel.

Mum made some tea while they waited for the vet to arrive.

'I'm sorry I've been such a nasty neighbour,' said Mrs Hutchens. 'It's just that I'm so used to being overprotective

towards Bambi. But it's no excuse and I'm sorry.'

'You *have* been really rotten,' said Jack honestly.

'Jack!' said his mum, shocked.

'It's all right,' smiled Mrs Hutchens. 'I think I deserved that. I *have* been rotten. But from now on, things are going to change. And I want you to know that you and Hercules are both welcome in my garden at any time.'

Jack gasped and made himself cough. Then Bambi yapped and Hercules jumped out of the box and limped across the kitchen to get a special cuddle. Jack was good at cuddles. And so was Hercules. They couldn't have dreamed of a better ending if they'd tried.

**If you enjoyed reading this story,
look out for _Hercules 3: Treasure Hound_
– here's an extract to whet your appetite!**

'You're in a hurry this morning,' said Mum suspiciously, as she pulled up a chair to the breakfast table.

Jack was busy cramming toast into his mouth and trying to tie both his laces at the same time.

Hercules was eager to help, but only succeeded in making matters worse.

'Gerroff,' mumbled Jack through a mouthful of eggy toast. 'You've just made me tie both trainers together!'

'More haste, less speed,' said Mum. 'What's the big rush, anyway?' She glanced at her watch. 'If you've got a train to catch,' she joked, 'the next one's not due out from the station for another half an hour. And, seeing that your Dad will be driving it, it won't be going anywhere just yet, since he's still upstairs getting ready.'

Jack's father was the manager at Sallyford Station but he still took the _Pacific Princess_ out on her two daily excursions along the scenic coastal route. The old steam train was a popular tourist attraction and ferried holidaymakers between the summer resorts of Fentown and Rilport.

'It's the school project,' mumbled Jack from under the table, with Hercules busy washing his ears. 'I'm meeting CJ at Sandy Spit again to look for fossils.'

'Really?' said his mum. 'When I spoke to her yesterday, CJ told me that she had a football match this morning.'

Jack's head popped up from beneath the table, followed by that of his partner in crime, Hercules.

'Oh, the match,' he said quickly. 'That's not until this afternoon. It's been postponed. Put back to three o'clock, I think.'

Jack hated telling lies. He knew that once you started lying you had to carry on, or you got caught out. Even *little* fibs had a funny way of tripping you up. But it wasn't as if he was *really* being dishonest about something. It was just that he was sworn to secrecy.

Meeting CJ was the first excuse he had thought of. Jack could hardly tell his mum he was meeting a nutty professor who was going to entrust him with a special secret. A secret linked with treasure, spies and a mysterious enemy! It was the kind of thing that only happened in books or on TV. No way could he risk Mum saying no.

Jack finished his chocolate milk, jumped up from the table and headed for the back door, with Hercules trundling along behind him.

'Bye, Mum. See you later.'

'*Jaack*.' This was Mum's special way of calling him when he had been caught out or was in big trouble.

Jack stopped in his tracks with his hand frozen on the doorknob. Hercules gulped and threw himself down on to his belly, paws folded across his nose.

'Haven't you forgotten something, Jack?' asked Mum.

The lead, thought Jack. *I've forgotten Herc's lead. Phew.* For a moment he thought he'd been rumbled. 'Thanks, Mum.' Jack snatched the lead from its hook on the far wall and hurried back towards the door.

'Ja-ack!'

Oh no. The long slow 'Jack' again. *She's torturing me,* he thought.

'Don't you need *this,* Jack?' Mum was holding up Jack's schoolbag with all his project things in it. 'Might come in handy!'

'Thanks, Mum.'

This time, Jack shot out through the back door so fast that even Hercules had a struggle to keep up – and he was lightning on legs!

The pace continued as Jack grabbed his bike and took off through the gate, along the lane and down The Tunnels.

Hercules, the atomic wonderdog, put his little legs into overdrive and raced behind like a greyhound.

'It'll all probably just turn out to be a load of nonsense, Herc,' said Jack as they pulled up at the shingle ridge of Sandy Spit. 'Professor Brimble's probably not even going to turn up.'

To cool himself down after his mini-marathon, Hercules started panting. His long pink tongue lolled from his mouth as he listened to his young master rambling.

'I'll give him five minutes,' said Jack. 'No more. If he doesn't turn up, we'll go and watch CJ's match after all.'

'Wuff,' agreed the little dog. He scrabbled up the ridge after Jack as he pushed his bike to the top and stashed it in a narrow gap, against the cliff-face.

'Wuff, wuff, wuff!' Hercules had raised himself up on to his hindlegs and was barking at something above their heads.

Jack shot a glance skywards and saw a head duck back from the shoulder of rock. He stared hard. That was three times now! Someone up there was definitely keeping a watch on something. But who? And why?